HAUNTED
HOUSE

There was a noise downstairs and a prickle of fear ran down my spine. It was a soft and echoing noise, such as a ghost might make on walking through a door. In my mind's eye I saw it hovering downstairs in the dusty hall, a pale and ghastly figure, arms raised in full haunting mode.

I held my breath and went cold all over, for I could hear soft footsteps on the staircase. One step . . . another . . . closer and closer.

I hunched myself down, my hoody over my face and my eyes screwed shut. I wished I hadn't come. I didn't want to hear a ghost after all, and I especially didn't want to see one.

Filled with horror, I heard the bedroom door opening and my name being called. "Jake. . ." the creature said in a chilling whisper. "Jake. Where are you?"

Coming soon:

Plague House

HAUNTED
HOUSE

MARY
HOOPER

■SCHOLASTIC

Scholastic Children's Books,
Commonwealth House, 1–19 New Oxford Street,
London, WC1A 1NU, UK
A division of Scholastic Ltd
London ~ New York ~ Toronto ~ Sydney ~ Auckland
Mexico City ~ New Delhi ~ Hong Kong

First published in the UK by Scholastic Ltd, 2003

ISBN 0 439 97723 1

Printed and bound by Nørhaven Paperback A/S, Denmark

10 9 8 7 6 5 4 3 2 1

For Richard,
who supports Brentford FC and
helped me with all the football bits

CHAPTER ONE

It was Jenna who saw the dog first, but it was me who worked out that it was a ghost. I mean, my sister's a bit dippy but she's not actually raving. If she said she saw a dog – a little brown and black beagle – and I didn't, then it had to be a ghost.

We'd only been living in Bensbury a few days when she first saw it. Three days, and it already felt too long. We'd just moved from a suburb near London with a football pitch, swimming pool, skateboard park and millions of people, to Bensbury, where there was nothing to do and about twelve people. Well, OK, I'm exaggerating a bit, but there was no pool or pitch, and the school Jenna and I had to go to in September was a six kilometre bus ride away. What there was in Bensbury, apparently, was something mysterious called the "quality of life".

"The quality of life," Mum kept saying to us – like whenever we complained about there being nothing to do – "is so much better in the country. You'll find things to do in good time. You'll have *hobbies*. Nice country hobbies."

She said that on our first Monday morning, when Jenna and I were staring out of the window of the shop and moaning, sighing and gnashing our teeth.

"You just have to look for things to do." She shook her head. "I don't know – I went to all the trouble of having twins so that you'd be company for each other. Why can't you just play together nicely?"

"*Play* together?" I snorted. "What, like with fuzzy-felt or something?"

"As if!" Jenna said.

Jenna and I had never really knocked around together – never had to, because we'd always had our own mates before. In the holidays she'd have been doing girly things with them while I'd have been outside kicking a ball.

"You could always help me in the shop," Mum

added. She was in charge of Bensbury's only general store and post office, and we were living in two rooms at the back of it and three over the top. OK, it was bigger than our flat in town which overlooked the gas works, but give me gas works over green fields any time.

And as for helping Mum – well, that depended. I didn't mind refilling the glass case containing chocolate bars and quite liked stacking packets of biscuits, but didn't want to do anything with boring household stuff you couldn't eat.

At nine o'clock Mum rolled up the blind which hung over the post office counter, ready for business. "Why don't you two both stand by, ready to be helpful?" she said. "You can say good morning to people, Jenna, and open doors for them, and you, Jake, can pack their shopping and carry things to their cars."

"I'd rather go outside and practise my silky right foot crosses," I said. "Just in case a talent scout comes along."

Jenna laughed scornfully. "You think you're so good, don't you? You think you're Beckham."

"As matter of fact I *am* pretty ace on the pitch."

"In your dreams. . ."

"Twins!" Mum said warningly. And then she added, "Anyway, no ball games on the green, Jake. It says so – there's a notice out there."

"Oh, brilliant," I said bitterly.

And so, having nothing else to do (Mum already having banned football from the shop) Jenna and I both slouched behind the counter. I positioned myself near the chocolate raisins. Later, I thought, a few might accidentally fall out of the jar and into my mouth.

"I'll introduce you to the customers," Mum said, "and when they tell us their names, try and remember them so that the next time you see them you can use them. We want to be accepted here and it's polite little touches like that which will make all the difference."

"Oh, joy. . ." I said.

"Polite little touches. . ." Jenna added in an agonized voice.

So, we slouched there and waited and waited, but as hardly anyone lived in the village, customers weren't exactly pouring through the door fighting to be served. In fact, it was nearly ten o'clock before anyone came in at all. In the meantime Jenna and I occupied ourselves by pressing our noses against the glass door, one

4

inside and one outside, and seeing who could make the worst, most horrible face at each other. Mum was out the back adding up columns of numbers and didn't know what we were doing until she came out and saw that the door had gone all breathed-on and sticky, and then she stopped us. After that, we just stared out of the window at . . . nothing. Or practically nothing.

Outside our shop was a grassy road, and on the other side was the village green, which had a few trees and bushes and a small pond (and also a notice saying No Ball Games, apparently). On the other side of the green was a pub called the Unicorn; scattered around were some lines of cottages and, further off, a church. If you went down one of the roads off the green you came to an estate of modern houses, and then some farms and a huge house called the Manor.

That was about it, unless you counted cows and stuff, and I didn't. It was the sort of cosy, flowery village you get a photo of on a calendar; one of those places where nothing ever happens. The cottages were mostly of the thatched, twee sort – apart from one on the far side of the green which looked really out of place. It might sound funny put this way, but if the other houses were all cosy and smiley, this one wasn't. This one was frowning. It was bigger than the two on either side of it and was dark and run-down, with blackened windows and a front garden tangled with overgrown trees and creepers. I pointed it out to Jenna and we agreed that there was something weird about it, but it wasn't until later that we discovered exactly what this something weird was.

As the customers started coming in that morning I cheered up a bit because we'd got an excellent game going. Mum had told us that a good way to remember people's names was to think of a word which described them and which was similar to their actual name, so when you saw them again their appearance or their manner would remind you of what they were called. Like, one of the first people to come in was Major Butley, who was a big man with a fat, pink face.

"Bumface Butley," I said immediately after he'd gone out.

"Good one!" Jenna said.

The next man in was Mr Green, and when we said, "Good morning," he said, "Is it?" and then started going into one about moles that were messing up his garden with molehills, how there were no daily bus services any more and how the village hall was an eyesore.

"Grouchy Green," Jenna whispered to me.

After that we had quite a laugh. Mrs Snape (who was either snorting into a hanky the whole time, or sniffing) became Snotty Snape, Miss Hall (great big teeth and hair up in a ponytail) became Horseface Hall, hairy Mr Gibbs became Gibbon Gibbs, bald Mr Slade was Slaphead Slade. Miss Ratcliffe, who wore a tatty bit of fur around her neck and had a face like a ferret, became Ratty Ratcliffe and enormous Mrs Hugo was Mrs Huge-o. There were also a few ruder ones which we didn't tell Mum about.

It was surprising how well it worked to help us remember, actually, because later in the day when we saw the people we'd named, either in the shop or about the village, Jenna or I would say, "There's Moaning Mowlem," or "There goes Piggy Pinder."

About five o'clock that first day, just as Mum was about to pull down the post office blind, a new woman rushed in. She introduced herself as Mrs Scudder and said she worked as a carer for several of the older residents in the village, including an old Mr Dudley who lived in the row of cottages diagonally across the green from our shop.

The woman looked all of a mess, hair everywhere, her blouse sticking out of her skirt and a smudge of paint down one cheek. "Mrs Scudder is *scatty*," I whispered to Jenna, and she nodded in agreement, grinning.

"Mr Dudley's a lovely old chap but he's on his last legs, I'm afraid," Mrs Scudder said to Mum. "He can't get out now, he's practically bedridden, so I look after him and do all his little errands."

"Mr Dudley is *doddery*," Jenna whispered.

It seemed that Mr Dudley needed some milk and teabags and other stuff, and as Mrs Scatty Scudder was in a hurry to get home (she was sure she'd left the cooker on), Mum told her that Jenna and I would deliver Mr Dudley's groceries.

It was just then, as we came out of our shop with a cardboard box full of stuff for Doddery Dudley, that Jenna saw the dog.

She pointed across to the row of cottages. "Ooh! Look at that dog sitting outside there," she said. "So sweet! I *love* beagles."

"You love anything with four legs and a woof. Or four legs and a miaow," I responded wittily.

"I especially love beagles!" she said.

I looked where she was looking, but couldn't see a thing.

"Beagle?" I said, mystified. "What are you talking about?" I looked up. "D'you mean eagle?"

"Of course I don't mean eagle, you dumbo!" Jenna said. "I think I know the difference between a dog and a bird."

"I can't see any dog."

"There!" She pointed again, and then she said, "Oh." Just like that.

"What d'you mean – *oh*?"

"It disappeared," she said in a stunned voice. "Just disappeared into thin air. One minute I was looking at it, the next it had gone."

I shook my head despairingly. "Sometimes I wonder if you were dropped on the head as a baby."

For once she didn't come back with something, but just stood there, staring at where the not-dog had been.

We walked on to Doddery Dudley's – who was so doddery that we weren't allowed to knock at his brass lion's head door-knocker in case it disturbed him. We had to leave the cardboard box outside ready for Scatty Scudder to take in when she came back at seven o'clock to do his supper and get him ready for bed.

"I really did see a dog," Jenna said as we came out of Mr Dudley's gate. "It was sitting right outside here on the grass."

"Well, it isn't now."

She frowned. "Where did it go, then? I mean, it didn't run across the green, or we would have seen it. Maybe it ran down a hole or something. They have those in the country, don't they? Animals dig them – badgers and rabbits live in them."

"Dunno," I said. I didn't know a thing about the country. Cows might have dug holes, for all I knew. But it was then that I thought of what it might be. "Perhaps it was a ghost dog," I said.

Jenna looked at me. "What?"

"Bet it was!" I said, suddenly feeling more interested in the whole deal. "I've just read a book about a ghost dog. It was a werewolf and it used to come in the night and bite people so that they died of a horrible disease." I made a blood-curdling noise as I said this, and leaped at Jenna's neck.

"It didn't look like a werewolf," Jenna said, brushing me off. "More like a cute fluffy toy."

"Well, it would do – living here," I said. I wasn't sure right then whether I truly believed it was a ghost, but thought I might as well pretend it was. It would make the place more interesting. "It was *definitely* a ghost dog," I added.

"Well, OK, just supposing it was," said Jenna, "How come I saw it and you didn't?"

"Hmm. . ." was all I said, because I didn't really have any answer to that.

As we walked back towards the shop a man came trudging towards us scowling at nothing. It was warm, but he was wearing a thick tweed jacket and had a weird hat with earflaps on it. "Who's this?" I whispered to Jenna.

"Grouchy Green," she whispered back, then she nudged me and said in a false, polite voice such as Mum likes us to use, "Hello, Mr Green!"

"It's a lovely evening, Mr Green," I added.

"*Is* it?" said Grouchy Green, scowling deeply at us. "And who might you be?"

"We're from the shop. You met us this morning."

"Ah, yes, the pigeon pair," he said, and before we could work out what this meant, added, "And it *might* be a nice evening, but only for those that don't live next door to haunted houses."

Jenna and I looked at each other, and then I turned and caught up with him. "Excuse me," I said politely, "where is it you live, exactly?"

"Back of the green," he grunted, pointing. "Next to *that*."

I looked over to where he was pointing, which was the frowning sort of house I'd noticed earlier. "Oh. *That* one," I said.

He grunted and started walking off again, but Jenna was there next to me by then, as nosey as ever. "Haunted? Is there a ghost there?" she asked him.

He gave her a sharp look. "I hear noises. Thumpings. Screams when there's no one there. A ghost is what I calls it."

"And has the house always been like that? Always haunted?" I asked.

"I've been living here forty-three years," Grouchy said, "it's always been haunted and it gets worse around this time of the year. If you ask me, there are unquiet spirits in that house. Restless souls."

When he said this I got really excited: unquiet spirits, restless souls. *Brilliant*.

"Do you know why? Why the . . . er . . . spirits are unquiet?" I asked.

"Oh aye," he said. "It was way back – Victorian times, so they say. A blacksmith married a young French girl and they went to live there, but she disappeared on the day after the wedding."

"Where did she go?" Jenna asked.

"No one knows," Grouchy said. "And they say he – the blacksmith – went alooking for her, then died of a broken heart when he couldn't find her. Now he haunts the house searching for her, moaning like anything. People have tried to live there – twenty years back Mr Starr tried it – but they never stay."

"Wow!" I said. "Fantastic."

"Oh, it's not, Jake." Jenna put her concerned face on. "I think it's really sad."

"You may think it's sad," said Grouchy, "I think it's blasted annoying. Weeping, wailing and carrying on and keeping good folk from their sleep. . ." And saying that, he shuffled off, muttering to himself.

"Just think," Jenna said, staring across the green. "There's a haunted house here. . ."

"And a ghost dog," I added.

"So maybe it won't be quite as boring as we thought."

"Hey," I said, "Mum wanted us to find something to do, didn't she? She wanted us to have a hobby. Well, this is going to be it. We're going to be ghost hunters."

CHAPTER TWO

I flicked up the ball neatly and chipped it from one side of the green to the other.

"No ball games on the green," Jenna said.

"If you look, you'll see that it's not actually *on* the green," I said, looking to see where it had landed. "That whack sent it right *across* the green so that it reached the other side." I adopted my *Match of the Day* voice. "What a ball! One of the greatest cross-field passes this season!"

Jenna just sighed. "How sad it is," she said, "that your entire life is just one extended game of football."

"Too right!" I said, punching the air. And then I looked at her pityingly. "God, it must be awful to be a girl."

After having a few more snaps at each other, we crossed the green and reclaimed my ball, then walked towards the sinister-looking house. This, spookily enough, was looking even *more* haunted since we'd heard about its history. In the garden of a cottage alongside it a woman was bending over, planting something. This cottage stood on the other side of the haunted house to Grouchy Green's; it was a twin of his.

Jenna leaned over the fence to say hello to the woman and when she turned round we saw that it was Ratty Ratcliffe. The old girl didn't have a lot going for her, actually, looking to be at least half rodent, with a long pointy nose, sticking-out teeth and a quick way of turning her head and looking at you through little darting black eyes. All she needed was whiskers and you'd have been hard pushed to tell her apart from something the cat brings in.

We went through polite good afternoons and Ratty did the usual, "Oh, are you twins?" routine, and then said, "How nice. A pigeon pair!"

Jenna and I looked at each other. Why were this lot on about pigeons the whole time? "Miss Ratcliffe," I said in my best speaking-to-wrinklies voice, "Miss Ratcliffe, we spoke to Mr Green earlier and he was telling us all about the house next door to you."

Jenna nodded towards it. "He said that it's haunted. Is that right?"

"Well, of course it isn't!" Ratty said briskly.

"Oh," I said. I was dead disappointed. "He seemed really sure it was."

"Did he? Well, what a silly, morbid old man he is — always complaining about something! It's just a creaking, squeaking old house with a lot of trees that make noises in the wind. And anyone who thinks it's haunted wants their brains tested!"

"But what about the story he told us?" Jenna asked.

"About the blacksmith and his bride," I added. "Is that true?"

Ratty nodded. "That bit's true all right," she said. "I've done quite a lot of historical research on this village and I know the story."

"Can you tell us more about it?" I asked, reluctant to give up on being a ghost hunter quite yet.

Miss Ratcliffe fixed her ratty eyes on the horizon. "It was about a hundred years ago when the local blacksmith met a young lady from France. He asked her to marry him and she agreed, so her family bought that big house next door for them to live in. There was a fancy wedding, and a party to which all the village were invited, but the next morning when the blacksmith got up, he found that his bride had disappeared."

"But where had she gone?" I asked.

"Back to France!" Ratty said promptly. "She decided she didn't love him after all and went back to her family. End of story."

"So did he stay on in the house and die of a broken heart?"

"Not at all. A few years later he married a nice sensible local girl who was a farmer's daughter, and took over her family's farm."

"But what about the weeping and wailing that Mr Green hears?"

"Just trees creaking, branches shaking and wind whistling down chimneys – nothing else at all! Mr Green is talking out of his hat."

"But why hasn't anyone else bought that house, then?" I asked.

"Isn't it because it's haunted?" Jenna put in.

"Of course not," Ratty said. "It's because the

French family who owned it never came over to live in it, nor put it up for sale. Travel was difficult a hundred years ago – maybe they intended to come over but never quite made it. Then I suppose over the years the family died out and the house got forgotten."

Jenna and I were both quiet while we took this in, and I felt a bit deflated. If we weren't going to be ghost hunters, what were we going to do with ourselves? I thought longingly of my mates back in London, of our pitch near the gas works. What were they doing now? Had they got a striker to replace me? Bet it was that Wayne Mooney; he was *rubbish*.

Jenna nudged me. Being her twin, I knew what this meant.

"Can we go and look in the house?" I asked Ratty.

"Go and look? Whatever would you want to do that for? Don't tell me that sensible children like you believe that silly old story of Mr Green's."

"No, of course not!" I said. "We're just. . ."

". . .studying insects!" Jenna said quickly. "House spiders and so on. We thought there would be some good examples in a neglected house like that."

"There probably would be," Ratty said, nodding. "And I've got some encyclopaedias on insects and arachnids if you'd like to borrow them."

We looked at her blankly.

"Spiders," she translated. "You did say you were doing a study of them?"

"Yes, and we'll just get off and do it now. Thank you very much!" I said.

Ratty went back to whatever it was she'd been doing and Jenna and I walked towards the haunted house.

"What d'you think?" Jenna said to me.

I frowned deeply. "Bit of a choker. Grouchy says it's haunted, Ratty says it's not."

"We don't have to believe her, though, do we?" Jenna said. "She's very sensible and straight so maybe she just doesn't see and hear these things. Maybe old Grouchy is sort of extra-sensitive to things."

"You mean he's psychic?" I said.

"Yeah," she said. "And I was thinking that – if it was a ghost dog – maybe that's why I saw it and you didn't. Maybe *I'm* psychic too."

"Maybe," I shrugged in an offhand way, as if I didn't care one way or the other. What I was thinking, though, was that if she was psychic, I should be as well – or was that a bit of a girly thing to be?

We stood outside the haunted house looking up at it, and I decided that if ever there was a prize for the most sinister-looking place, this would win hands down. Thick dark green ivy had grown all over its walls and twisted chimneys, and there was furry brown moss on the roof. It had pointed spooky windows like you get in churches, but they were so filthy and overhung with ferns and things that you could hardly see them. The front garden was full of brambles, roses and big climbing plants which had grown up over the house, and the whole place looked deeply mysterious and as if it could have been in some sort of old fairy tale.

"It's like the garden that grew up round Sleeping Beauty's castle!" said Jenna.

I frowned. "Trust a girl to know something like that," I muttered. I looked all around us. No one was watching. "Shall we go in?"

"Of course."

And so (leaving my ball outside) we went through the front gate. Or over it, actually, because it was so rusted up it would probably have fallen to bits if we'd tried to open it. And then we fought our way up the pathway through the brambles, using a bit of wood to push at the undergrowth which got in our way.

We reached the front door and tried the handle, but it was locked. We then had to fight our way over a side gate and through a fallen-down greenhouse, with stinging nettles as high as your head and brutal bushes with long thorns set on tearing you apart.

When we eventually reached the back door we found that it was locked as well, but then Jenna found a little window at the side where the glass was broken. We removed a pointed and deadly shard of glass, squeezed ourselves through and found ourselves in a small room with shelves all round it and thick dust and dead insects over everything.

My heart was beating very fast and I was suddenly just a bit startled about what we'd found ourselves doing. We hadn't *done* things like this in London. There hadn't been any haunted houses or ghost dogs there.

"This is the pantry," Jenna whispered. "It's what they used to have before fridges. To keep the food in."

I sniffed. The air felt damp and stale. I could smell mice, too – I'd had two white rats once and they'd smelt the same. I took a deep breath. "Let's have a look round, then."

It was a good job it was a sunny day or we wouldn't have been able to see a thing in that house, but as it was, rays of sun somehow found their way through the jungle outside and the grime on the windows, and lit the place to a dusty mugginess.

The next room was the kitchen, which wasn't very interesting. It just had a big old sink filled with spiders and dirt and a few beaten-up shelves. There was no furniture, table or chairs or anything else.

"Yuck! It's all so filthy," Jenna said.

"What, actually, are we looking for?" I asked.

"Dunno," she said, and then she said, "Oh, I know: *clues*. That's what people always hunt for."

"OK," I said. "And that would be clues as to. . .?"

". . .whether this house is haunted or not. And if so, who or what is haunting it."

We crept through the kitchen into the hallway, which was empty, with dark-brown painted stairs leading upwards. Off this hall were two big, high-ceilinged rooms, both with greeny-black windows and sooty, rubbish-filled fireplaces. There was also a chair with all the stuffing falling out of it.

Jenna looked around. "Just think!" she said suddenly. "Once in the olden days these rooms were full of people all celebrating the wedding of the blacksmith and the French girl. There would have been a big wedding cake on a table there –" she pointed – "and someone playing music on a fiddle, and dancing, and all the village people would have been dressed in their best. The French girl would've been wearing a long shimmering dress and had flowers in her hair. . ." Her eyes were closed. "I can almost picture it! I think I *am* psychic."

"I think you're cracked," I said.

We went upstairs. In one room there was a broken-down single bed and a tumble of blankets, as if a tramp had been living there. There had also been a fire in the room's small fireplace. I bent down to look at what remained of the charred wood. "There was a fire here not too long ago," I said. "There's a bit of the *Daily Mail*. Sports page, too. I wonder who was top of the. . ." And then I suddenly realized. "Hey, I bet that's the answer. It's not a ghost at all, just some old tramp who dosses here sometimes and lights fires to keep himself warm. That's who Grouchy Green hears."

Jenna looked at me. "He said moaning and wailing, though."

I shrugged. "Maybe he's a miserable tramp. Maybe his team lost."

"Oh, do shut up about football." Jenna shook her head thoughtfully. "Tramps don't wail and cry," she said. "They might talk to themselves, or sing if they're drunk, but they don't wail. No, I just think there's something wrong here." She screwed up her eyes. "This room . . . it doesn't feel right."

She began to pace around a bit, frowning, so I did the same. I wasn't going to let her be psychic all on her own. Whilst pacing, I suddenly noticed something by the door and bent down to take a closer look. The floorboards were filthy, covered in dust and debris from where part of the ceiling was coming down, but on one of them there were some faint blotches. "What d'you think these are?" I asked Jenna.

She came over and we traced the line of drops

from inside the room to the top of the stairs. "I think it could be blood," she said.

"So the tramp cut himself."

She shook her head. "This is from *years* ago. And see where the boards are lighter here? I bet someone's tried to scrub the marks off."

We looked outside the bedroom door, but the marks stopped at the top of the stairs. When we went down and looked in the hall, though, we found two dark spots outside a small door under the staircase.

"I bet that leads to a coal cellar," I said. "Like the one in gran's house."

We tried the door, but it was nailed shut. And then Jenna gave a yell and pounced on something on the wooden floor, digging it out with her fingernail.

"It's a little seed pearl," she said, holding it up. "It was hidden in a crack in the floorboards; I just happened to see it gleaming." Her eyes went all strange and faraway. "I think it's from the bride's wedding dress. . ."

CHAPTER THREE

We didn't say anything to Mum, of course, either about the ghost dog or the haunting business, because we knew she would have gone off on one about us breaking into an empty house. Jenna stuck the little pearl on to a piece of sticky tape, though, and slept with it under her pillow that night, saying she thought she might dream of the blacksmith and the bride and find out what had happened. She didn't, though (so she couldn't have been *that* psychic, I thought).

The following day Scatty Scudder rang Mum and asked if we could pop down to Doddery Dudley's cottage with a few household things that she needed: bleach and soap powder and stuff, so Mum packed them in a box and off we went, me dribbling my football along the ground in front of me.

Halfway there it dropped down the kerb and, as I turned to flick it up with one quick movement of my trusty right foot, Jenna gave a gasp. "That dog!" she said. "He's outside Doddery Dudley's again!"

I turned in an instant. "*What?*" I said, looking where she was pointing. "I can't see anything! Where is he exactly? What's he doing?"

"He's got a red lead in his mouth and his head on one side. He looks really cute!"

I frowned deeply, squinting towards where she was looking. This was so annoying. How come she could see things, *feel* things, and I couldn't?

"Oh, no! He's disappeared again!"

We started running, reached Doddery's gate and looked all around. We even looked for any sign of rabbit holes (or pig holes or whatever) big enough for a dog to have gone down, but there was nothing to be seen.

We stood there, baffled. "This whole village is *completely* weird," I said.

"You're telling me," said Jenna.

I parked my ball at the gate and we tapped at the door. Scatty Scudder opened it and beckoned us inside. "Bring the stuff through to the kitchen," she whispered.

The sitting room had that funny closed-in smell that old people's rooms have, as if it needed to have its windows opened for about a year. It was crammed with furniture: two plush red sofas, a battered leather chair, three little tables and a long brick mantelpiece full of pictures, china and bits and pieces.

Jenna, seeing some photographs and getting an attack of the noseys, stopped to look at them. I carried the box of stuff through and plonked it down on the kitchen table.

Scatty Scudder, living up to her name by having her blouse done up on the wrong buttons and only one earring, smiled at me. "You're good kids!" she said. "Are you twins, then?"

I scowled at her; she was speaking to us as if we were about eight. "Yeah," I muttered.

"Bless! A pigeon pair!"

"Yeah, right," I said. I walked back through the sitting room where Jenna was still standing by the fireplace looking at the photographs. She was holding up a photo of a short, trim little man wearing a striped cotton jacket and red bow tie. "Is this Mr Dudley?" she asked.

Scatty came up. "Yes, there's the dear old chap in his heyday," she said. "Very dapper, he was. Always dressed immaculately – whether he was shopping, going out for an evening at the Unicorn or walking his dog."

When she said the word "dog", Jenna and I looked at each other.

"Not now, though," Scatty went on. "Poor old devil never gets out of his pyjamas now."

"What breed of dog does he have?" Jenna asked.

"*Did* he have, you mean? Whatever d'you want to know that for?" she asked, and without waiting for a reply went on, "Don't ask me. Some little black and brown one." She reached behind a china ornament. "There's a photograph here somewhere. Yes, here it is."

She gave Jenna another picture of Doddery. Next to him, sitting looking up at his master as if hoping for walkies, was a beagle.

Jenna and I nudged each other. "Wow," I said under my breath.

"That's the one!" Jenna said. "It's even got the red lead in its mouth."

"Yes, that's old Wellington," Scatty said. "Inseparable, the two of them were." She put the photos back and ushered us to the door, obviously wanting to get rid of us. "Tell your mother I'll settle up at the end of the week, will you?"

I knew what Jenna was thinking but I wanted to say it first. "Where's Wellington now that Mr Dudley can't walk him any more?"

"Is he still in the village?" Jenna asked.

"Oh no," the woman said, "poor old Wellington died a couple of years back."

I heard Jenna gasp under her breath.

"It upset Mr Dudley dreadfully," Scatty went on. "He started getting poorly then, and never really recovered. Someone gave him a budgie but it wasn't the same." She lowered her voice to a whisper. "He's on his last legs now, poor old chap." She propelled us through the door. "Right, I must get back to work. Goodbye, twins!"

"Well!" Jenna said as soon as we were outside the door.

"Can you see the dog now?"

She shook her head.

"And it was definitely a beagle?"

"Course!" She shook her head reflectively. "But maybe it's just a coincidence. It could be another beagle . . . someone else's. Maybe it's a dog who used to come round here and play with Wellington and it keeps coming back to look for him."

I nutmegged the ball through Jenna's legs as I thought about things. "That doesn't explain why it keeps disappearing," I said. "Or why I can't see it and you can. No, it's got to be a ghost dog."

"So we've got a haunted house here *and* a ghost dog," she said. "Not bad for starters."

We walked back to the green and sat down. A bit embarrassing, really, being seen around with your sister all the time, but there was totally no one else to go round with. There was practically no one under eighty in the whole village.

"The thing is," I said, "what do we do next? It's all very well finding these ghosts, but what do we do with them – just leave them drifting about the place?"

Jenna frowned. "No, we have to investigate them and then . . . there's a word. . ."

"Exercise them!" I said.

"Not quite – not take them for a run. *Exorcise* them," she corrected.

"I knew really."

"We have to discover the reason they're

earthbound. Why the dog keeps coming back – and why the blacksmith keeps wailing around the place."

"And how do we do that?"

"Dunno!" she said. "Go back to the house again, I suppose. Get more psychic feelings and then act on them."

"Hmmm," I said, not really liking the idea of her getting all the psychic feelings and me getting nothing. "We ought to go there at night, really."

She gave a girly scream. "I wouldn't dare!"

I shrugged. "It's only a house. Ghosts can't hurt you."

"They can scare you!"

"It's only at night that ghosts walk and weep and wail, though – and how can we investigate properly if we don't hear any moaning and wailing?"

Jenna gave a shiver. "Well, you can count me out."

"OK, then," I said. "I'll go on my own!"

Her eyes widened. "You wouldn't really go over there at night, would you?"

"Course!" I said carelessly. "When you've faced the agony of watching your team in a penalty shoot-out, that's nothing."

"Go on, then," she said. "Go tonight at midnight!"

"Right," I said, thinking to myself that I might not be psychic, but I was pretty damn brave.

By twelve o'clock that night I'd changed my mind about being brave. How had I got myself into this – being forced into seeking out ghosts in the middle of the night? I was a goal hunter, not a ghoul hunter.

I was quite hoping that Jenna had fallen asleep so that I could forget about the whole deal, when she tapped at my door and came in waving a torch.

"D'you still want to do it? Have you changed your mind?" she asked in a whisper.

"Course not," I lied. I rolled out of bed and pulled on my jeans and a hoody over my pyjamas. "And I've already got a torch."

"This is a spare one," she said, handing it over. "You ought to take it in case yours goes out." She knelt on my bed. "Look, I can see the house from here, so you can signal me. Two flashes of the torch means you've seen a ghost, three flashes you've heard one, four. . ."

"Never mind all that," I interrupted. "You don't think I'm going to hang around signalling to you with a ghost breathing down my neck, do you?"

"All right then. But if you're not back by morning, I'll send a search party."

It was pretty easy to get out of the house. I just went down, unbolted the side door and was away. As I crossed the lane I glanced up at my bedroom window and waved to Jenna, then pulled my hoody further over my head so that if seen, I wouldn't be recognized. I didn't know who might recognize me, mind you, because there was no one about. The Unicorn was closed and most of the houses were in darkness, there was just a small street lamp alight in front of our shop.

I felt quite good sprinting across the green. I'd hardly done any training since we moved, but it didn't show because I was still dead speedy. There was nothing to be scared about, I reasoned. What was the worst thing that could happen? Some old ghost would howl at me. Well, at least then we'd know what we were up against.

Silent as a cat-burglar, I climbed over the front gate of the haunted house and made my way round to the back, my hoody taking the worst of the scratchy thorns. I shone my torch through the window which led into the pantry, then climbed through and stood there for a moment, listening. I thought I heard a noise but it was just my heart beating, hard and fast. It wasn't necessarily because I was scared, I told myself, just excited.

I went through to the hallway and up the stairs, wondering if Jenna could still see the light from my torch. I remembered then that I'd meant to leave my pillow humped under my duvet so that if Mum came in she'd think I was still there, but seeing as Jenna was perched on my bed anyway, that didn't really matter.

At the top of the staircase I went into the bedroom on the right – the one with the bloodstains, and it was then, sitting down near the fireplace, that I got a severe attack of the creeps. It was so quiet. So horribly quiet. There were no clocks ticking or water pipes gurgling, no swishing of trees or even any far-off traffic noise, just my heart thumping away.

But at least there was no wailing of ghosts, either.

Willing myself to stop shaking, I stood my own torch on the floor and put on Jenna's, too. I wanted all the light I could get.

But maybe ghosts only came out in the dark?

Too bad, I thought. Not even for a chance to play in the England under-14s was I going to turn off those two torches and sit in complete darkness.

How long would I have to stay?

Until I heard something, I supposed.

But then if I didn't hear anything . . . would two minutes be enough?

There was a noise downstairs and a prickle of fear ran down my spine. It was a soft and echoing noise, such as a ghost might make on walking through a door. In my mind's eye I saw it hovering downstairs in the dusty hall, a pale and ghastly figure, arms raised in full haunting mode.

I held my breath and went cold all over, for I could hear soft footsteps on the staircase. One step . . . another . . . closer and closer.

I hunched myself down, my hoody over my face and my eyes screwed shut. I wished I hadn't come. I didn't want to hear a ghost after all, and I especially didn't want to see one.

Filled with horror, I heard the bedroom door

CHAPTER FOUR

"Jake!"

"Arrgghhh!" I buried my face between my knees. I wasn't going to look. *I was not going to look*. If I ignored it, if I pretended that I didn't believe in it, then perhaps it would just drift back into the nether regions it had come from.

"Jake! It's me." The ghost shook my shoulder. "Sorry. You didn't really think I was a ghost, did you?"

I lifted my head from between my knees. Then I opened my eyes very slowly.

Jenna stood there. "Sorry," she said, giggling. "I really gave you the frights, didn't I?"

"Wh-what?"

"You thought I was a ghost!"

My mouth and throat had gone as dry as a bit of sandpaper and I coughed a bit, trying to compose my voice so that it didn't come out like a mouse's squeak. "Nah!" I said. "I knew it was you."

"You looked pretty done-in to me. . ."

I tossed my hood back. "I'm cool," I insisted. "Haven't heard anything, haven't seen anything." I swallowed hard. "What you doing over here, anyway?"

"I couldn't stand not knowing what was happening."

"Talk about nosey."

"So I found the torch that mum keeps in the shop and followed you over." She sat down beside me. "Now that we're here, what'll we do?"

"Dunno," I said. "Just chill out a bit, I s'pose. Watch and wait."

So we did. We played I Spy, but this was pretty limited seeing as there was nothing much in the room once you'd done the two "d"s – dust and dirt. We then went through everyone in the village that we'd met, going over their names and testing each other on them.

By one o'clock we were bored and yawning.

"Shall we go home?" I asked Jenna.

She nodded. "We've done our best."

"This doesn't mean there aren't ghosts here," I said, "just that they aren't around tonight."

"Exactly." She began to get to her feet, and then she looked at me and gasped, her eyes round and startled. "I can feel something strange in the air. . ."

"Yeah. Right."

"No, honestly!" Her face had gone pale in the torchlight. "It's gone cold in here. And there's a faint noise . . . like someone whispering or crying." She sat down again, much closer to me. "Jake! Something's coming up the stairs."

I would have accused her of trying to get me going except that she was shaking and sounded so stressed out that I knew she wasn't. "Let's get out of here, then," I said.

"No, Jake. Wait." Jenna put out her arm to stop me getting up. "Just sit here a moment. It's all right. I don't think it'll hurt us."

"How d'you know that?" I said. "Are you suddenly the world's authority on ghosts?"

"Ssshhh. . ."

She went all quiet, closing her eyes and putting her head to one side as if she was listening. I did

41

the same thing but all I could hear was her breathing.

"What is it?" I said. "What's going on?"

"Ssshh. . ." Her eyes sprung open suddenly and she stared across the room. "Oh!"

"Oh – *what*?" I hissed, getting annoyed.

She closed her eyes again for a moment, and then she said, "It's OK. It's gone now."

"Are you speaking to me or to the ghost?" I asked irritably.

"You," she said. "The ghost's gone down the stairs again."

"Well, was it really one? What was it *like*?"

She hesitated. "It was really odd," she said after a moment. "Not like I thought it was going to be – not like those ghosts on TV that look like someone wearing a sheet. It was more . . . more fragile than that. Not so much a figure, more a sort of blurry lightness. More atmosphere and mistiness than anything solid."

"Perhaps it was a moonbeam or something," I suggested.

"No. It was a ghost," she said decidedly, "and it was crying to itself."

"Was it the ghost of the blacksmith, d'you think?" I asked, thinking that this didn't sound very macho for a big strong man who'd spent his life banging horseshoes around on anvils.

She shook her head. "It wasn't him, it was his wife." She grabbed my shoulder. "Don't you see – it's not the ghost of the blacksmith that old Grouchy hears wailing about the place, but the ghost of his bride!"

"Yeah. Right," I said again, because it suddenly sounded utterly bizarre: ghosts, blurry light shapes – she'd be seeing little green men next. "If it was just a blurry shape, how come you knew it was her and not him?"

"She had a long shimmery dress," she said. "And she . . . the ghost . . . is terribly unhappy, Jake. It's not so much a scary ghost, as a *scared* one."

"What d'you mean?"

"She's frightened. She's frightened of *him*."

"Ah." I was silent, thinking deeply, while we went downstairs and climbed out of the pantry window. Then I said, "So, if her ghost really is haunting this house and it's not just you messing about. . ."

"Honestly it's not!" she protested.

"That means she never went back to France after all. She died here in England."

"And now she's earthbound and stuck here in this house," Jenna said.

"And we've got to release her. . ."

We slept until eleven o'clock the next morning, until Mum stood at the bottom of the stairs and hollered up to us both that she needed help – *now*! – with some deliveries. These were: a registered letter going to the Manor, a box of groceries for Piggy Pinder, who apparently had a nasty head cold and didn't want to go out – and, more interestingly, a big parcel for Mr Starr, who lived in a row of tall houses behind the church. We'd never seen Mr Starr but Horsey Hall had told us that he was a taxidermist. This didn't sound very interesting – we thought he was some sort of cab driver – until Mum told us that it meant he was a person who stuffed animals.

"What d'you think is in this box of his, then?" I asked Jenna, picking it up and seeing if it rattled.

"Dead wildlife?" she suggested. "Otters and penguins and things ready to stuff?"

I shook my head. "They'd have to be refrigerated or they'd go off," I said. "Maybe it's glass eyes."

"No," Jenna said. "It's much too big. You could get about a thousand eyes in that box."

"Maybe it's the actual stuffing stuff, then. Straw or whatever."

"We'll ask him," she said.

But we didn't get the chance right then, because when we rang his bell – which played a little tune we couldn't quite make out – he shouted that he couldn't come to the door because he was busy manipulating a squirrel.

"Yuck! Wonder what *that* means," Jenna said.

"We're from the post office. We've got a parcel for you!" I called through the letter box, but he shouted back for us to leave it on the step.

Disappointed, we did so. "We didn't even see him to name him," I said as we went home.

"Bet he looks really strange," Jenna said. "Bet he's a weirdy beardy."

"Stuffer Starr!" I said.

Jenna clapped her hand to her mouth. "I've just remembered," she said. "Didn't old Grouchy say that Mr Starr – I mean, Stuffer – moved into the haunted house at one time?"

"He did!" I said, and we immediately turned round and began walking back.

I rang his bell, and we thought that it sounded

like "*All things bright and beautiful, all creatures great and small...*" so we pushed it a couple more times to find out. There was a bellow of rage from inside the house.

"I told you to leave the parcel on the step!"

"We can't!" I lied. "Not allowed. We need a signature."

There was a long drawn-out groan. "You'll have to wait!"

So we did, and couldn't resist ringing the bell a couple of times more and it definitely *was*.

"That's awful," Jenna said, between giggles. "All creatures great and small – and he's *stuffing* them!"

When Stuffer came to the door he looked grumpy – and as mad as a mallard. He was a tall man, with wiry grey hair standing up like he'd had an electric shock, and long straggly grey sideburns. He had more hair protruding from his nose and even, as we saw when he turned his head, from his ear holes. It was like he'd been over-stuffed himself and it was poking out everywhere.

"I don't usually have to sign anything," he grumped. "Where's the form, then?"

"Ah," I said. We hadn't thought of this. I

turned to Jenna. "Where is it?" I asked pleasantly. "I hope you haven't lost it."

"Why me?" she said indignantly.

"We must have left it on the counter," I said, giving her a meaningful raised-eyebrow look. "If you go back and get it I'll ask Mr Starr those questions."

She gave me a glower, but she went.

"This is most annoying," Stuffer said, breathing hard down his nose so that his nose-hair moved. "I have two dozen squirrels to get ready for a Wildlife in Winter show and they're all at a very critical stage."

"She won't be a moment," I said. I cleared my throat. "Mr Starr, we've only come to live here recently and we were . . . er . . . talking to Mr Green about the house next to him. He thinks it's haunted."

"So it is," Stuffer said.

"Really? How d'you know?"

"Well, it was a long time ago now, but my house was being re-roofed, so I thought I'd move in there for a few weeks. Couldn't stay there, though."

"But did you actually see anything?" I asked eagerly.

He frowned. "What do you want to know for?"

"Scientific research," I said quickly. "We're doing a special project."

He shook his head. "No, I didn't actually see anything – but I heard noises. Crying and wailing is what I heard."

"And . . . er . . . d'you remember what time of the year you were living there?"

He frowned. "I can't remember that. It was more than twenty years back."

"Summer or winter?" I asked helpfully.

"Ah," he said, "it was summer because it was warm. June, maybe July."

"Ah," I said. *It always gets worse at this time of year*, Grouchy had told us.

Jenna came back. "Here it is!" she said, passing a piece of paper and a pen to Stuffer.

He looked first at one side and then the other. "This paper is completely blank."

She nudged me.

"We . . . er . . . have to fill in the details afterwards," I said.

Late that afternoon I was outside practising my dribbling on the circuit I'd devised for myself around the green. I had to go round twice, then cross the green bouncing the ball on my head. This, I assured Mum, was *not* ball games on the green, for I was so skilled that at no time did the ball actually fall and touch as much as a blade of grass (this is what I told her, anyway).

While I was on the other side of the green, Jenna came out of our shop and began walking along the road. At the corner, she bent down and started peering at something – a flower, I thought – walked past it, then came back again two or three times to speak to it. One or two oldies went by and said something to her, and when they'd gone she began talking to the flower again in a completely mad way. After a bit she saw me staring at her and ran over, trying to tackle me for the ball and failing miserably.

"What are you on?" I said. "I saw you over there talking to yourself and looking half-mad."

"I was talking to Wellington," she said.

"What?"

"The beagle. He was sitting near Doddery's gate. The thing is, I can see him, and he *knows* I can see him."

I balanced the ball on the end of my toe and

then sent a screamer bouncing on to someone's wall. "You're talking tripe."

"I'm not! I was watching him. He was sitting there quietly outside Doddery's gate, his red lead in his mouth, and when I came close he looked up at me and he *knew* I could see him. I bent down to pat him – though I couldn't feel any fur or anything – and he barked, which made him open his mouth and drop the lead."

"But what about the other people walking by?"

"They couldn't see him, so they didn't pay any attention to him and he didn't pay any attention to them."

"Hmm," I said. I frowned. "I'm not sure what all this means. Ghost dogs . . . what are we supposed to do about them?"

"Exercise them?" she said, and we both laughed.

"Really, though – I dunno," I said. "Maybe he'll just stay outside Doddery's house and wait for him for ever."

"Maybe," she said. "But I think that's really sad. I wish there was something we could do to help. . ."

CHAPTER FIVE

The next morning Jenna and I were both in the shop when Ratty came in. I was busy looking at the chocolate raisins and wondering if Mum would notice that the level of the jar had gone down drastically, so didn't take much notice of her. Mum packed a couple of things into Ratty's trolley, then called over to me, asking me to climb the ladder in the shop to get down a packet of brown sugar.

Hastily putting the lid back on the raisin jar, I pushed the ladder along to the right place and climbed up. When I reached the top shelf, though, I found there were a few different sorts of brown sugars. I looked at the names, then called out to ask Ratty, "Soft brown, demerara or muscovada?"

She didn't reply.

"What *sort* of brown sugar?" I asked again.

She still didn't say anything. Didn't even *look* at me, so I gave Jenna a meaningful everyone-here-is-bats look, and she went over to speak to her. "Jake wants to know what sort of brown sugar," she asked Ratty.

Ratty jumped. "Sorry, dear. Was someone speaking to me?"

No, I make a habit of sitting on ladders and talking to myself, I felt like saying, but instead I said, "Up here, Miss Ratcliffe! Soft brown, demerara or muscovada?"

She pointed her nose towards me in a ratty way. "Sorry, dear, I can't hear you. I forgot to put my hearing aid on this morning."

I gaped at her and, just like in the cartoons, a lightbulb flashed on and off in my head. I bet that was why. . .

I got all three sorts of sugars, brought them down the ladder and then put them in front of her on the counter. "Soft brown, demerara or muscovada?" I bellowed, making Mum jump out of her skin.

"Demerara," said Ratty.

Jenna took a deep breath. "Miss Ratcliffe!" she

shouted. "Do you wear your hearing aid at night?"

"Whatever d'you want to ask her a question like that for?" Mum muttered.

"No, I don't," Ratty said. "I find I have a much better night's sleep without it on. The battery digs into me, you see."

As Mum put Ratty's stuff into her shopping bag, Jenna came over. "So that's why she doesn't hear any ghosts," she hissed.

I nodded. "I worked that one out for myself."

Ratty paid and I dived to open the door for her. "Thank you, Miss Ratcliffe!" I bellowed. "And a ghost morning to you!"

"Good morning to you, too!" she beamed.

That afternoon I decided to make myself scarce. Jenna had to do something girly with Mum, something involving making a cake for the village fête, so I decided to go and do a bit of investigating on my own.

I really wanted to go to a newspaper office, because you're always hearing about people going to their local newspaper to find out about things, but I discovered that Bensbury didn't have a local newspaper as such, just half a page of news in the *Waverley Gazette*. This was published weekly in Waverley itself, which was about thirty kilometres away, but I couldn't go there because the buses only went on Tuesdays and Thursdays, and this was a Wednesday. This was what it was like living in the country.

Instead Horsey Hall (I'd been asking her about buses) directed me to the library, which was open on Wednesdays and Saturdays in a small room off the village hall.

When I first went into the poky old place I was a bit sneery about it because, looking at the state of it, I didn't for one minute think I was going to find anything useful there. The place we'd lived before had had this fantastic modern library where you could borrow videos and CDs as well as books. Surprisingly, though, I found loads of stuff, because they had newspaper reports going way back about anything that had happened in the village. This covered small things like lost dogs, weddings and washing being stolen off a line, to a fire which had burned down the Manor. There were also records of all the memorials and gravestones in the churchyard, leaflets produced at various times for festivals and fêtes, and lists of births, marriages and deaths.

"The whole village through the years is here," said the old boy in charge of the place. He was Mr Fichard and as he had a bald head and droopy, open mouth he immediately became Fishface.

I told him who I was and where we lived, ("Ah yes, you're one of the pigeon pair," he said) and then started investigating straight away. Grouchy had said to us that the blacksmith had married the French girl in Victorian times and, cursing this queen for having lived so long, I started trawling through the newspaper reports. All of them had been carefully cut out and stuck into scrapbooks and I read through about ten years' worth. Then I decided it would be just my luck to work through sixty years only to find out it had happened at the *end* of her reign. Crossing my fingers, I moved on a few scrapbooks to the year she'd died and prepared to work from there backwards. I was dead pleased when I found it almost straight away.

The date was 1900 and the cutting read:

Well-known Bensbury blacksmith Albert Daniels will be married to his French sweetheart, Amelie de Bois, tomorrow, Saturday 15ᵗʰ July. Amelie recently came to this country from France, having held a position as French governess for the children of Lord and Lady Bothy at the Manor.

Their marriage will be officiated by the Reverend Griffiths at Bensbury Parish Church, and afterwards there will be a celebratory wedding breakfast at the happy couple's new home on the green, which was a wedding present from the bride's family. All villagers are invited to attend this.

This was all there was on that page, but quickly turning to the next I found:

STRANGE DISAPPEARANCE OF FRENCH BRIDE

Last week we were happy to report the forthcoming wedding of blacksmith Albert Daniels to Amelie de Bois. The ceremony itself took place at two o'clock, the day was bright and sunny and Miss de Bois looked radiant in a long cream dress which was entirely covered in miniature pearls.

I stopped here and thought about the tiny pearl that Jenna had found stuck down a crack in the floorboards and which she carried around in her pocket now. So it *had* been from the bride's dress. . .

Miss de Bois wore a circlet of flowers on her head, and carried a bouquet of white stephanotis and lilies, and there were two small maids in pale green silk. A lavish wedding breakfast was provided for friends of Mr Daniels and Miss de Bois, and dancing continued until late.

The following morning, Sunday 16th July, dawned as bright and sunny as the day before, and it was at ten o'clock that Mr Daniels's fellow blacksmiths thought to surprise the couple by going to the house and playing a rousing tune on their fiddles under the window. They found Mr Daniels alone, alas, and in a state of some distress. Once the poor man could speak, he told them that his wife had decided she did not wish to live on foreign soil and had returned some hours before to her native France. It is thought she walked into Waverley and hailed a passing *hackney carriage to take her to the coast so that she could catch a ferryboat.*

Mr Daniels has let it be known that he will return all wedding presents, but at the moment does not wish to make a statement on the matter.

Even more excitingly, there was a photo. It showed a tall, brawny man with dark curly hair, buttoned into an old-fashioned jacket. On his arm was a girl, small and slim. Her dress was shimmery – because of the pearls, of course – and she had her hair up with flowers stuck in it. She was looking up at the blacksmith in a soppy way, but he was just staring at the camera and looked like a bit of a miserable git.

I stared at it for ages, and then I took a photocopy of both pages on the ancient copier behind the library counter. After that I started looking through 1901, and then 1902 and 03, hoping to find further news of Daniels the blacksmith. But it wasn't until 1904 that I found, in the lists of births and marriages:

The family of Mary Burns, of Sheepwash Farm, Appleton, are happy to announce her marriage to Mr Albert Daniels, Blacksmith. The ceremony took place quietly in Waverley on 3ʳᵈ April. The couple will make their home in Appleton and take over the family farm on Mr Burns's forthcoming retirement.

I went home full of everything and dead pleased with myself. Wait until I told Jenna...

"Got loads of things to tell you!" I said, as I entered the shop. I waved my notebook and pointed towards upstairs for her to come and join me.

"What are you two up to?" Mum asked from behind the grille of the post office. "And what sort of things?"

"Just..."

"We've got a hobby," Jenna said. "You wanted us to have one and now we have."

"And what is it?" Mum asked suspiciously.

"Ghost hunting," Jenna said promptly, and I gave a disgusted look. What had she blabbed for? Why didn't she ask Mum to join us for tea in the haunted house while she was about it?

Mum just laughed, though. "You and your jokes!"

"Why d'you tell her that?" I hissed at Jenna when we got upstairs.

"Because," she said, "if it all comes out later and she finds out we went out in the night, at least we can say that we tried to tell her what we were doing."

I could see a point to this, but didn't admit it. Anyway, I was dying to tell her what I'd found out and show her the photo. The photocopy of the newspaper wasn't that good, but you could see what the dress was like and Jenna was practically speechless when she read that it was all-over pearls.

"I knew it," she said, getting out the little pearl and rolling it between her fingers. "When I saw her as a ghost, she still had the dress on." She stared at the photo for some time. "I don't like that blacksmith," she said finally. "There's something cruel about his eyes. And I don't like the way he's staring at the camera, so full of himself. If she *had* gone back to France I wouldn't have blamed her a bit."

"But. . ."

"But I don't think she did. I think they had a row, and I think he murdered her."

"Blimey," I said, startled. "That's a bit drastic."

"I've just got this feeling about it. A bad feeling. And then there's those marks on the floor. I'm sure they're bloodstains. . ."

"But what happened after – did he hide the body and no one ever found it?"

"That's what I think," she nodded. She looked at the newspaper report again. "D'you know what next Saturday is?"

I shrugged. "The fifteenth of July. Four weeks to the start of the football season and it can't come quickly enough."

"No," she said, "it's exactly one hundred years ago to the day of their wedding."

"Yeah! You're right!"

"So. . ."

"So we'll have to go over to the house that night and try and help her. Find out why she's still haunting the place and try to release her."

"Oh, is that all?" I said. "You're speaking as if we release tortured souls from their earthly captivity every day of the year."

"Well, we can have a go."

My sister surprises me sometimes.

CHAPTER SIX

It was all very well us deciding to be a ghost's best friend and release it from its earthly bonds, but on the run-up to Saturday we did wonder what we were letting ourselves in for. Suppose the ghost didn't want to be released? Suppose it turned nasty? What if it turned into one of those ghosts that moved stuff around the room or threw things at your head? On a more ordinary level, suppose someone outside saw our torches lighting up the house and called the police, and we got done for breaking and entering?

But, as I said to Jenna, if we were going to be proper ghost hunters we'd just have to put up with any flak, so at 12.15 on the night of the fifteenth July there we were, sitting ourselves down on the bedroom floor of the haunted house. If the ghost came along at the same time as it had previously, then we had about forty-five minutes to go.

"I hate sitting on this dirty, hard floor," Jenna said for about the fourteenth time, shifting first this way, then that. "I meant to bring a cushion."

"Huh!" I said. "Compared to the sufferings of a ghost condemned to walk the earth for a hundred years, it's hardly a big deal, is it?"

We emptied our pockets, putting everything on the floorboards between us. I had a spare torch battery, two handfuls of chocolate raisins and a penknife. Jenna had Travel Scrabble. We'd talked a bit over the past few days about what we were going to bring with us and I said we ought to have a tape deck to record any wailing. Jenna, though, said that as I couldn't hear it, it wasn't likely that anything would be recorded. Same went for taking pictures – if she could only see a vague bit of a shape and I couldn't see anything, it was hardly going to be worth taking. Besides, neither of us had cameras and Mum's was so complicated no one had ever managed to use it.

"Help yourself to a raisin," I said to her generously, and we amused ourselves for a while throwing them up into the air and trying to catch them in our mouths. After that we got out the Scrabble board, but couldn't be bothered to play. It wasn't often you found yourself in a haunted house exactly a hundred years to the day after the crime, and playing Scrabble didn't seem quite appropriate.

"What are we actually going to do when we see the ghost?" I asked.

"When *I* see her, you mean," Jenna said a bit smugly.

"Whatever," I shrugged. I didn't know if I wanted to be psychic myself, anyway. You never heard blokes talking about things like that in the changing rooms. On the other hand, it might be a good thing for a footballer to be psychic, then he could tell when someone was going to send him a brilliant fifty-metre cross-field pass before it happened.

"I mean, do we say some special words, or throw something at her, or what?" I went on.

"Oh!" she exclaimed. "We should have bought some holy water with us. Aren't you supposed to sprinkle a ghost with it?"

"I think that's a vampire," I said. "I've seen it in the films. You hold up a cross and a string of garlic – they hate garlic – and that stops them in their tracks, then you sprinkle holy water on them and they frizzle up to nothing."

"Right," Jenna said. Another few minutes passed. "Shall we play I Spy again?" she asked.

"Nah," I said, yawning.

She giggled. "I was just thinking how funny it was last week when you were here on your own and you practically had kittens when I came into the room because you thought I was a ghost."

"Garbage!" I said. "I knew it was you."

There was a snigger from Jenna and then another silence.

"If Stuffer Starr runs out of material to stuff his animals with, d'you think he uses hair and nose clippings?" I asked.

"Don't be disgusting."

I had a flash of inspiration. "I know what'll pass the time – I'll explain the offside rule to you," I said. "It's very interesting and girls always find it difficult to—"

Suddenly, from downstairs, there was a terrible scream. I mean, a horrible, blood-thirsty, *terrifying* scream, and we both jumped.

"Did you hear that?" she asked shakily.

"Yeah..." I said, and *I* was speaking a bit shakily too.

A moment later I also felt the temperature drop suddenly, and saw dust swirl in the moonbeams, and felt something – like a shadow, but an indistinct, light-coloured shadow – cross the room and cower somewhere under the window.

Jenna clutched me. "She's here . . . the ghost is here," she said in a trembling voice. "And she's trying to get away from him!"

Another moment passed and a dark shadow came into the room; a colder presence. "What's happening now?" I asked in an urgent whisper, because though I could kind of sense things, it seemed like I was sensing things through Jenna and not directly, as she was doing.

"He's come after her and he's got something like a poker in his hand. She's run across the room and she's trying to get out of the door, but he's hitting her. . ." Jenna gasped and shrank back against me. "Now she's got blood on her face and she's fallen by the door and isn't moving. The place she's fallen – her head is right where those bloodstains are!"

An instant later I asked, "Now what? Can you see? Is he still here or what?"

Jenna shook her head, straining to see. "Everything's gone much more blurry. But I can hear noises – and now there are thuds going down the stairs. Thud . . . clump . . . all the way down."

"It's her body," I said. I swallowed hard. "Her body is thumping on each step. He's dragging her downstairs."

After a moment Jenna said the thumping had stopped, and we just sat there, neither of us speaking. I was clenching my teeth hard to stop them from chattering.

A bit later Jenna asked in a whisper, "Where d'you think he's put her body?"

"Dunno," I said. "The garden? No, the cellar. I bet he's put her down in the cellar!"

We sat there, still not moving. I didn't fancy going down to that cellar. No way. Not tonight. I was hoping Jenna wasn't going to suggest it.

"What shall we do? Shall we tell the police, or what?" Jenna asked.

"What would we say?"

"Well, just tell them. . ."

"What? That we're ghost hunters, and we've solved a hundred-year-old murder that they didn't even know about? Oh yeah, I can just see them going for that."

"So, what, then?"

"I think we ought to see the job through," I said. "We don't really know anything for definite. We haven't got any proof yet."

"You mean we should come over here in daylight and check for a body?"

I nodded. "I'll bring something to get that cellar door open. And if we see anything suspicious down there, *then* we'll go to the police."

We stayed a bit longer, trying to talk about ordinary things and get back to normal, because we both felt very weird and very spooked. Eventually, though, we got up and went downstairs and found that everything was as it had been when we'd come in: the hall was silent and dusty, the sitting room was still bare and creepy – and the cellar door was still nailed up.

We went home and to bed, but I felt too wound-up to sleep. I was also wondering whether – because I'd sensed a ghost – I was psychic. Or was it only through Jenna being psychic, and us being twins, that I'd felt it at all?

Maybe we'd made the whole thing up between us, had let our imaginations run away with us (Mum was always saying things like that). We had no proof yet. *That* would have to be found in the morning. . .

CHAPTER SEVEN

I woke up about eight when I heard Mum moving about downstairs. A moment or two later, before I'd hardly got my eyes open, Jenna came running into my room.

"Something really strange has happened!" she said.

I groaned. "I'm not ready for another something strange yet."

"Listen to this! I woke up a couple of hours ago because I heard a dog barking."

"You don't say."

"It was about six o'clock – just getting light. And I looked out of the window and what d'you think I saw?"

"Surprise me."

"Doddery Dudley!" she said.

I must admit that this *did* surprise me. "*What?*"

"He must have recovered from his illness or whatever it was he had."

"Are you sure it was him?"

"Course!" she said. "He was short and trim and he was dressed just like he was in that photo Scatty showed us, with a striped jacket and bow tie. He was walking across the green as perky as anything."

"How could he have recovered, though?" I said. "I thought he was on his last legs. Are you sure you weren't dreaming?"

"No, I. . ." She suddenly gasped, "Oh! I've just remembered. I went straight back to sleep after that and I've only just thought of what else I saw." She stared out of the window across the green, as if she was trying to see him again. "You see, Mr Dudley was carrying Wellington's lead. The red lead."

I frowned. "Really?" I asked. "You sure?"

"And that's not all: Wellington was running in front of him. He was chasing along with his tail in the air, and every few moments he'd look back at his master and bark. . ."

Her voice trailed away, and the two of us just stared at each other. "There's something funny here," I said.

But before we could begin to work it out for ourselves, Mum came running up the stairs from the shop. "Glad you're both awake," she said. "I want you to help out this morning serving. We're bound to be busy."

"Why?" we both asked.

"Because people will be passing by and coming in for condolence cards and so on. And to order flowers too, I should think." She shook her head. "It's sad, really – even though we never knew him. He sounded like such a nice old chap."

Jenna gave me a wide-eyed look. "What's happened?" she asked Mum.

"It's Mr Dudley. Oh! Silly me. You don't even know about it yet."

"About what?"

"Well, Mrs Scudder went along to his place at seven o'clock this morning to get him up as usual and get his breakfast, but found the poor old man dead in his bed. She called the doctor, and he came straight round – he seemed to think that Mr Dudley had died shortly before Mrs Scudder had got there. I saw her flapping about outside and went out and spoke to her."

She went out again. "Must get ready for a busy day!" she said, leaving Jenna and I gawping at each other, utterly amazed.

"Wellington has been standing at the gate for weeks, waiting and waiting for him," Jenna said after a moment.

I nodded. "And today Doddery Dudley finally came out to go walkies." I thought of something and grinned. "Hey, maybe we should rename him Dead Dudley."

"Jake!" she said, giggling. "That's awful."

That was the nice part of the day. Sad, OK. But nice. Dog and master reunited after death. Had a nice ring to it.

The other part of the day wasn't so great.

We were both keen to go over the road to the haunted house, but the shop was really busy and Mum wouldn't let us out. For a start, it was pension day, when all the oldies queued up for their money, but even if it hadn't been, then the death of Doddery would have pulled them all in. Everyone in the village gathered in little groups inside and outside the shop: Ratty and Horsey and Stuffer and all, chatting about "his passing" as they called it, remembering the last time they'd seen him, wondering what Scatty was going to do now she didn't have him to mind and saying that the man had never been the same since his dog had died.

While they chatted they remembered things they wanted to buy, or discussed who would provide the funeral tea and if they ought to buy something towards it, or popped in to order their flowers through Mum.

"Pity about Mr Dudley, but look at the money they're spending – every cloud has a silver lining, eh?" I whispered to Mum, but she told me to *ssshhh*, adding that she didn't know how I could say such a thing.

She finally let me and Jenna out about two o'clock, by which time the entire village had met in our shop and everyone had said anything there was to say about Mr Dudley, his dog, his house, his garden and all else to do with him.

"I'd love to tell them what I saw this morning," Jenna said wistfully as we walked across the green to the haunted house, our torches in our pockets.

"They'd just think you were mad," I said.

"As mad as they are, you mean?"

"Almost. We'll all probably get that batty if we stay here long enough."

We trod the by now well-worn path around to the back of the house and entered by the same window. The whole thing, the whole ghost-hunting scheme, seemed ridiculous in the bright sunshine. Poker-wielding blacksmiths, disappearing brides, ghosts condemned to die over and over again? Yeah, right.

"Did we make it up?" I asked Jenna. "Who's to say that we didn't just sit upstairs in the gloom and talk ourselves into the whole thing?"

"You might have," she said. "I didn't. I heard it before, remember? *And* I saw Doddery Dudley and his dog."

I sighed. "OK," I said. "But if there's nothing in the cellar I'm not digging up the garden."

From up the sleeve of my hoody I drew out a claw hammer. It was the sort of hammer with – yeah, you guessed it – a claw on the end, so that you could dig out nails with it. It took me ages to get them out of the cellar door, though, because they were great big long ones and were rusted into the wood. I had to drag the old chair in from the front room to stand on to reach those at the top, and the door looked pretty bashed about when I'd finished.

"If ole Grouchy can hear us he'll think the ghosts have taken up DIY," I joked to Jenna, but she was standing by the window with a funny look on her face, and didn't reply. She'd found another little pearl, right by the cellar door, pushed into the wood as if someone had stepped on it, and she'd prised it out and was now staring at it thoughtfully.

"OK," I called as I got out the last one. "The nails are gone and I'm opening the door. Coming down there with me?" I added, speaking casually, as if I couldn't care less whether she did or not.

"OK," she said.

I tugged at the handle of the door, but it had been jammed shut for ever and didn't intend to open that easily. I pulled again, and got Jenna to pull me around the waist while I held on to the handle with both hands. Of course what happened then was it opened so suddenly that we flew across the room together and Jenna shouted that I'd trodden on her foot and broken her toe.

I didn't reply, because I was up and making my

way to the cellar door, shining my torch down the stairs.

"What can you see?" Jenna asked in a scared whisper, coming up behind me.

"Not a lot," I said.

"Any bodies?"

"None at all."

I stood on the top stair, shone the torch around once more, and then started making my slow and stealthy way down the stairs with Jenna one step above.

It *was* a coal cellar. Or had been at one time, because the walls were dark with coal dust and there was a pile of sooty old bags folded in one corner. It smelt damp – the mousey, unclean smell that was all over the rest of the house was worse in here.

"Look there!" Jenna had her own torch and was shining it on to a pile of packing cases and boxes. "I wonder what's in those?"

I jumped down the last three steps on to the cellar floor and the noise echoed around, hollow and strange, making me feel a bit spooked. It was cold in there, but I told myself that was just normal in cellars and didn't have to be anything supernatural.

"Look," Jenna said, going over to the pile of boxes. "There's a travel trunk at the bottom. Can you see what it says on the label?"

I shone my torch on to a tattered and faded white label stuck on to the side of the trunk. "*Mlle Amelie de Bois. Beny Bocage. Normandy. France,*" I read out.

"This is her trunk, then!" she said excitedly. "The one she used to bring her things over."

"What's so interesting about that?"

"Well, if she'd really gone back home, she would have taken this trunk with her, wouldn't she? Or at least sent for it later."

I nodded slowly. "But why didn't anyone find it here? Why didn't the police look into her disappearance?"

"Maybe they didn't have police then."

"Course they did!" I said scornfully.

"Well, maybe no one really bothered," Jenna shrugged. "Two people fall out, it's believed that one of them has gone back to France – and that's the end of it."

We looked to the big trunk and then back to each other.

"Shall we?" Jenna asked.

"I think we'll have to."

We pulled the boxes off the trunk. The first box was round and had once been shiny and white. It contained a faded blue hat with feathers all over it. The next was a packing case holding newspapers, the third held musty old clothes, folded and smelly. And something else...

As I gingerly put in my hand and felt about under the clothes, it encountered something bulky which I pulled out. It was a bundle of letters, yellow with age and tied with brown string. And they all had French stamps on them.

"Are they to her?" Jenna said, shining her torch over my shoulder.

I shook my head. "To him. Mister Albert Daniels."

"We must read one!" Jenna said, and she pulled at the string, which crumbled and broke, and took the top envelope from the pile.

The ink was faded and the writing spidery and old-fashioned. Hesitantly, screwing up her face to try and make out some of the words, Jenna read:

"Mr Daniels. We do not understand why you have not reply to our letters. We cannot believe that our dear daughter Amelie is dead. Please give us further details of the

accident you say occurred. Is it that she has been buried already? We understand that you cannot bring yourself to write of such things, but it is necessary for us to know of our dear one's last hours. . ."

"He must have told them that she died in an accident. I wonder why he didn't send her things back, though?"

Jenna shrugged. "We'll never know that." She put the letter on to the pile again. "We'll have to let someone see these," she said, and I nodded.

We'd now reached the large trunk at the bottom, which was made of dirty brown leather and bound all round with metal bands. It had once had a padlock on it, but it was now hanging off and almost rusted away.

I tried to lift the lid, but it had moulded itself to its bottom half and didn't want to come up. I handed Jenna my torch and, telling her to shine both of them down on to the trunk, used both hands to try and heave it open.

As with the door, the trunk lid came up in a sudden rush and so I was pitched forward and almost fell into the depths of it. Holding on to the rim, I stood back to recover my balance.

"It's her wedding dress!" Jenna gasped, for at first all we could see, shining in the light from our torches, was the vast shimmering of little pearls sewn on to the top of a dress.

A few seconds later we saw that a skeleton was wearing this dress, and that an eyeless skull wearing a circle of dead flowers was staring up at us. And then Jenna started screaming.

CHAPTER EIGHT

"You can't take footballs to funerals," Mum said patiently. "It's not right."

"We're not actually going to any funerals," I said, dribbling my ball around the shop counter and negotiating it between a pile of cake boxes. "We just want to hang around and have a look. See what happens."

"You don't *do* things like that at funerals. You go there to pay your respects to whoever it is that's died, you wear your best clothes and it's all very serious and solemn."

"They wouldn't be having one of those funerals if it wasn't for us," I pointed out.

"I know," Mum said, and she sighed. "But what I *don't* know is how it all happened – all this about a haunted house and a body in a trunk. I still don't know why you got involved in the first place. What were you doing over there? Why couldn't you have taken up fishing or rambling or something?"

"Jenna told you we had a new hobby and that it was ghost hunting. You didn't seem to mind."

"I thought she was joking! As if I would have allowed you to go into an empty house in the middle of—"

"Mum," Jenna interrupted, "what's a pigeon pair?"

"What?"

"That's what the wrinklies keep calling us."

Mum smiled. "How funny – I haven't heard that expression for years. It's what they call boy and girl twins."

"Oooh, you are a pigeon pair!" I said in an imitation-oldie voice, and that distracted Mum nicely from the telling-off we'd been about to get.

It had been five days since we'd discovered the "Bride in the Trunk" as she'd come to be called by the locals. As soon as we'd got home that morning and blurted out everything to Mum, she'd called the police and they'd zoomed up in two white cars, gone over to the house and found the bride for themselves. Following this, a line of blue and white tape had gone all round the place and we'd only been able to watch what was happening by hanging about outside and trying to squint in, or sitting up in my bedroom and fighting over whose turn it was to use the binoculars.

The police had now re-opened the hundred-year-old case of the disappearing bride. At least, they told us that they'd re-opened it, but it all sounded a bit woolly and Jenna and I thought that even if there had been a proper case once, more than likely all the paperwork had been lost years ago. The police had spoken to us about the noises we'd heard in the house, and also spoken to Grouchy Green, but the report we'd had to sign later hadn't said anything about there being a ghost in the house, or mentioned that we'd only been in there investigating because Grouchy told us it was haunted. We'd let the *Waverley Gazette* know the whole story, though, and there was going to be a full report in next week's paper which not only mentioned our names, but had photographs of us.

The police said it would take some time to investigate the case properly, and in the meantime they were going to try and find out if Amelie de Bois had any living relatives in Beny Bocage so they could let them know. I supposed that they were going to do the same thing with the relatives of the blacksmith, too.

"Nice for someone," I said to Jenna. "'Surprise! Your great-grandad was a murderer!'"

"Nearly as good as, 'Surprise! Your great-aunt was murdered!'" Jenna said.

In the meantime the local vicar had stepped in and insisted that the bride's remains have a proper burial, and it was taking place in the churchyard that afternoon, just after the funeral of Doddery Dudley. Anyone going to *that* would get two funerals for the price of one.

I flicked the ball up over my shoulder from behind (not a lot of people know that it takes considerable skill to do this) and assumed my *Match of the Day* voice. "He brings the ball neatly under control and takes it round the back of the display stand and. . ."

"You'll have that stand over!" Mum said. "Get outside!"

I got. Jenna was already on the green. She was

wearing a dress instead of her usual jeans and her hair was brushed.

"You ready?" she asked. "You are coming with me, aren't you?"

All across the green, people were leaving their cottages and walking towards the church. They had suits on, and smart jackets, and collars and ties.

I shook my head. "Nah. I don't fancy going to a funeral. I think I'll stay here and practise my ball control. Just want to be ready when the call comes from the scout."

"I want to see if *he* turns up," she said.

"Who?"

"Doddery Dudley. D'you think he'll go to his own funeral?"

I shrugged. "You let me know."

Grouchy Green came along wearing a dark suit and black tie. "Stupid time to have a funeral," he said to us. "Had to rush my lunch. Now I'll have indigestion all afternoon. Won't be long for the grave myself at this rate."

"But you'll be all right at home now, Mr Green," I said, "because there won't be any more ghosts wailing about the place at night and keeping you awake."

"That's what you think," he said. "You might have got rid of one of 'em, but there's plenty more in this village."

"Really?" Jenna and I both said together.

He resumed walking and Jenna fell into step alongside him. "Perhaps you could tell me exactly where. . ." I heard her begin.

I waited until she and everyone else had gone through the church gate and were out of sight, then I gave the ball a mighty thwack which sent it soaring across the pond. It was so mighty, in fact, that it whammed right into the sign saying No Ball Games, knocking it down.

So that was OK. I could play football on the green until the next ghost came by. And somehow, I didn't think that would be too long. . .

Look out for:

PLAGUE HOUSE

Jake and Jenna's next seriously spooky adventure.

When Jake and Jenna stumble across Corpses' Copse one day, they know there's something very sinister about it. Jenna hears children singing "Ring a Ring o' Roses", the chilling nursery rhyme that dates from the time of the Plague... The villagers warn the twins to keep away from the copse, but Jenna is sure that a ghost from the past desperately needs her help, and she *can't* say no...